KNOW THE SCORE

Hand-held games go anywhere, even out where the cactus blooms.
Author photo. Screen image™ © 1994 by Nintendo. All rights reserved.

KNOW THE SCORE

VIDEO GAMES IN YOUR HIGH-TECH WORLD

by Gloria Skurzynski

BRADBURY PRESS • New York
MAXWELL MACMILLAN CANADA   Toronto
MAXWELL MACMILLAN INTERNATIONAL
New York   Oxford   Singapore   Sydney

For Spike Alm and Danny Ferguson,
both champions

YOUR HIGH-TECH WORLD BOOKS
by Gloria Skurzynski

GET THE MESSAGE: Telecommunications
in Your High-Tech World
ALMOST THE REAL THING: Simulation
in Your High-Tech World
ROBOTS: Your High-Tech World

Acknowledgments

As always, this book couldn't have been created without the help of Lauren Thliveris, Jan Skurzynski, David Nolan, and, most of all, Ed Skurzynski. My most sincere thanks to Sam Palahnuk of Walt Disney Computer Software, Inc.; Mike McDonald and Kerry Wilkinson of MP Game Technologies, Inc.; Rich Robinson of Sony Imagesoft, Inc.; Traci McCarty and Chuck Vowell of Seta U.S.A., Inc.; Bill Linn of Sierra On-Line, Inc.; Sherrie Mennie of Nintendo of America, Inc.; Glenn Clapp of Evans and Sutherland; and Tom Byron of Spectrum HoloByte. Thanks also to the people who supplied information and photographs from Broderbund; Sega; W Enterprises; Battletech; MicroProse; 3DO; and Par T Golf. And my thanks to an editor who really knows her video games, Anne E. Dunn.

Bradbury Press
Macmillan Publishing Company
866 Third Avenue
New York, NY 10022

Maxwell Macmillan Canada, Inc.
1200 Eglinton Avenue East
Suite 200
Don Mills, Ontario M3C 3N1

Macmillan Publishing Company is part of the
Maxwell Communication Group of Companies.

First edition
Printed and bound in Singapore
10 9 8 7 6 5 4 3 2 1
The text of this book is set in 13-point Sabon.

Library of Congress Cataloging-in-Publication Data
Skurzynski, Gloria.
    Know the score : video games in your high-tech world / by Gloria
Skurzynski.—1st ed.
        p.   cm.
    Includes index.
    ISBN 0-02-782922-7
    1. Video games—Juvenile literature.   2. Video games—Juvenile
literature—Pictorial work.   I. Title.
GV1469.3.S58   1994
794.8—dc20   93-19470

CONTENTS

They're not exactly as different as night and day, but computer games (above) aren't the same as video games (opposite).
Author photo. Screen image by Spectrum HoloByte

Don't believe the title of this book, because it isn't only about video games. It's about computer games, too, and arcade games, and hand-held games. It's about the new games on compact disks, and the educational computer programs that make learning as much fun as game playing. This book tells how electronic games and programs are created—where the ideas come from, who puts them together, and how it's done, every step of the way.

71 percent of video-game players are boys; one-third of them are eighteen years old or older. When it comes to hand-held games like this Game Gear, the ratio changes to 56 percent boys, 44 percent girls.
Sega of America, Inc.

Video games are played on television screens. Their screen images are controlled through entertainment systems like Nintendo's and Sega's and NEC's. Says a game producer, "A video-game player goes for the thrills and chills, and wants a home game that's as fast as an arcade game. We call it the playability factor. Some people call it button-presses per minute."

Computer games are somewhat different. Mostly they're on floppy disks instead of cartridges, and they play on computer monitor screens. The programs get transferred from disk drives into the computer, and are controlled by computer keys, a mouse, or a joystick.

There are close to one hundred million households in the United States, of which one-third have computers. In addition, more than eighty million video-game systems, used *only* for game playing, are owned in the United States.

One advantage of video games is the size of their pictures. Computer screens rarely measure more than about 10 inches wide by 8 inches high—13 inches diagonally. A 27-inch (diagonal) television screen has four times the viewing area of an ordinary computer screen, so video-game images can appear much larger.

The pioneer of video games, PONG, was introduced by Atari back in 1976. With PONG, two people twirled knobs to knock the image of a ball back and forth across a television screen—an electronic version of Ping-Pong.

For the next ten years electronic games continued to be popular, but no one could have predicted the explosion that began in 1986, the year Nintendo brought Mario, the plumber, to America from Japan. Millions of kids rushed to buy cartridges so they could jump Mario across chasms and up and down different platform levels.

Computer screens are usually smaller—13 inches diagonally—than home television screens.
Author photo. Screen image by Spectrum HoloByte

If you're too young for a driver's license, test your road skills in an arcade.
Author photo. Game by Sega of America, Inc.

Then hand-held games appeared on the scene—any scene! Since they needed no wires or plug-in sockets, Nintendo's Game Boy, Sega's Game Gear, and Atari's Lynx could go anywhere (except underwater).

During the same period, all kinds of new arcade games sprang up across the country—simulators, holograms, interactive movies, motion-based rides, and virtual reality of two different kinds (see Chapter Five).

It was hard to imagine there'd be more to come, but by the end of 1992, another electronic-game revolution began, launched on compact disks. The disks look the same as the ones that bring perfect, buzz-free music to your stereo set, but they hold much more than just sound.

With CD-ROM (which stands for Compact Disk—Read Only Memory) and CD-I (for Compact Disk—Interactive), games look and sound very much like movies. They can talk to you—with human voices! Their musical backgrounds are no longer just electronic, but are fully orchestrated with real instruments. The graphics appear almost as clear as photographs; animation

The world's second video-game revolution arrived with CD-ROM and CD-Interactive.
Sega of America, Inc.

CD-I games can fill the largest television screens with sharp, detailed, moving, talking images that *you* control.
Philips Consumer Electronics, photo by Richard Foertsch

11

Packed with information, these disks let you discover puzzles, songs, music, and paint programs on unexpected pathways of a game.
Philips Consumer Electronics, photo by Richard Foertsch

moves smoothly; and actual movie footage shot with live actors can appear on screen as part of the action. This richness is possible because one compact disk can store as much signal information as 400 to 500 three-and-a-half-inch, high-density floppy disks. A game producer commented, "The difference in information storage is like a drinking glass versus a swimming pool. For designers, it's absolutely fantastic."

By 1994 video-game technology had taken two more giant steps. Sega of America, Inc., brought interactive video games to cable television, on the Sega Channel. And a company named 3DO designed a custom computer that delivers 50 times more graphics and animation power than 16-bit home entertainment systems. With full-color, full-screen, full-speed, full-motion images, the 3DO platform ("platform" means computer hardware and operating system) makes games look almost as good as movies. But instead of just watching, as in a movie theater, an interactive-game player gets to control what happens on the screen.

Advances in hardware and software have made games look and sound terrific, but those aren't the most important factors in a successful game. What makes a game a hit is its entertainment potential. A game with dazzling graphics, full sound, and great motion will still fall flat if it isn't fun to play.

Game makers know this. They like to brainstorm—share ideas—as they try to come up with the perfect design for next year's hottest electronic game.

In this classroom learning program, the student controls the pace, letting him master each step before he moves to the next.
Jostens Learning Corporation

Traci McCarty of Seta U.S.A. reads game suggestions sent in by young players. *Author photo*

IN THE BEGINNING

Chapter 2

All games start with an idea.

In a June issue of a video-game magazine, the following lines appeared: "Seta invites you, the *GamePro* readers, to invent some great ideas for the WIZARD OF OZ game play. If you have any suggestions, write to Seta U.S.A., Inc., Las Vegas, NV."

This was a most unusual invitation, and many young readers responded. Says Traci McCarty of Seta, "We got a lot of letters from twelve- to sixteen-year-olds. We even had good designs come in from kids as young as six, kids who had just learned to write and put their ideas down on paper." As the game designers began to create WIZARD OF OZ, they considered the mailed-in suggestions very carefully.

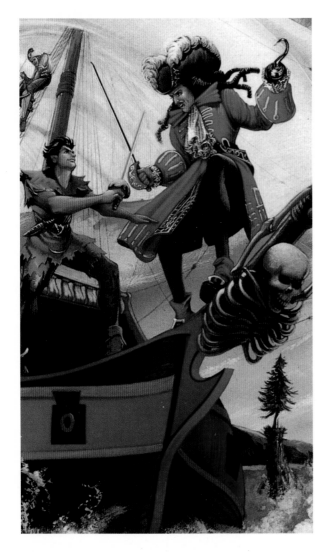

Though Peter Pan and Captain Hook have met many times on stage and screen, they needed a different concept for a video game.
HOOK™ and associated character names are trademarks of TriStar Pictures, Inc.

It can take twelve to eighteen months to make an electronic game, longer than it takes to make a movie. Rich Robinson, manager of game development at Sony Imagesoft, explains, "In the video-game industry, we go through five basic stages to create a game: define, design, program, test, and maintain."

To *define* means to state the concept of a game, in a paragraph, or even in a single line. For Sony Imagesoft's HOOK, the concept followed the premise of the 1991 movie and could be written this simply: "Peter Pan has grown up and Hook has kidnapped Peter's children. Peter's mission is to defeat Hook and rescue his children." Although the Peter Pan story already existed in many forms, it needed to be defined all over again when it became a video game.

Once a concept has been decided upon, the *design* phase begins. The design team must choose a genre (that means "classification"). A few genres have nicknames that describe them vividly: "hack-and-slash," "shoot-'em-up," and "punch-and-kick" or "kick-fu." Other, less violently named genres include mysteries, puzzles like TETRIS, role-playing games, action/adventure games, sports, mazes, simulations, and educational games.

After the genre has been chosen, the team must pick a perspective. Will the game have a sideview, like Nintendo's Mario games? Should it have the three-quarter-behind perspective that's used in a lot of racing games, where you actually view your car but you're not in it? (See the Game Gear screen on page 8.) Sega's arcade game VIRTUA RACING has a 360-degree (all the way around) perspective: if your car goes into a spin, you see a full circle of background.

Another element is point of view: whose eyes will you look through? In an interactive WILD KINGDOM game, you can watch a lion in the wild, or you can *be* the lion, and see the surrounding scene as the lion would see it. You can choose to be hunted, or to be the hunter.

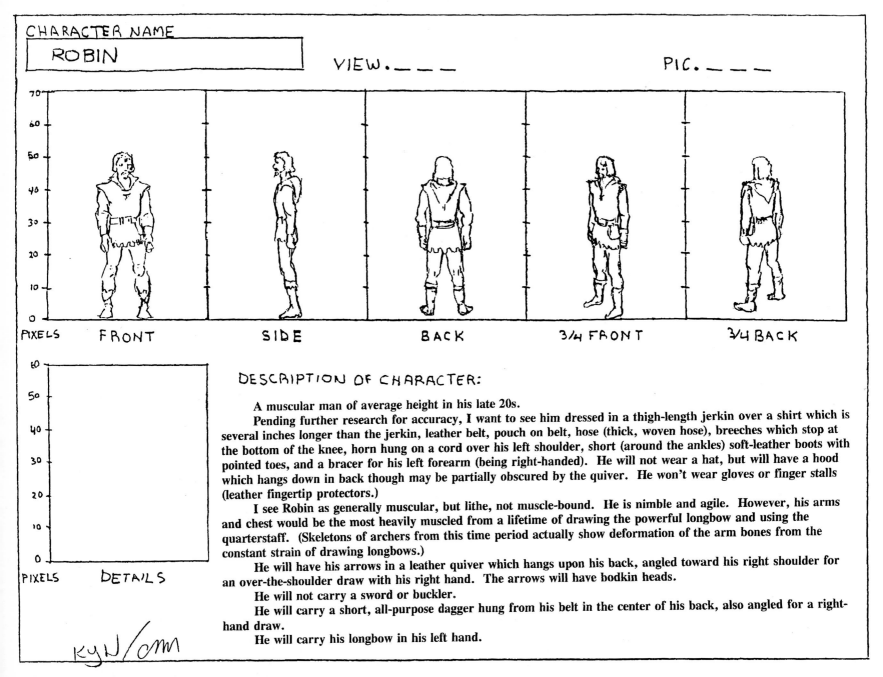

CHARACTER NAME

ROBIN

VIEW. _ _ _

PIC. _ _ _

FRONT   **SIDE**   **BACK**   **3/4 FRONT**   **3/4 BACK**

PIXELS

DETAILS

DESCRIPTION OF CHARACTER:

A muscular man of average height in his late 20s.

Pending further research for accuracy, I want to see him dressed in a thigh-length jerkin over a shirt which is several inches longer than the jerkin, leather belt, pouch on belt, hose (thick, woven hose), breeches which stop at the bottom of the knee, horn hung on a cord over his left shoulder, short (around the ankles) soft-leather boots with pointed toes, and a bracer for his left forearm (being right-handed). He will not wear a hat, but will have a hood which hangs down in back though may be partially obscured by the quiver. He won't wear gloves or finger stalls (leather fingertip protectors.)

I see Robin as generally muscular, but lithe, not muscle-bound. He is nimble and agile. However, his arms and chest would be the most heavily muscled from a lifetime of drawing the powerful longbow and using the quarterstaff. (Skeletons of archers from this time period actually show deformation of the arm bones from the constant strain of drawing longbows.)

He will have his arrows in a leather quiver which hangs upon his back, angled toward his right shoulder for an over-the-shoulder draw with his right hand. The arrows will have bodkin heads.

He will not carry a sword or buckler.

He will carry a short, all-purpose dagger hung from his belt in the center of his back, also angled for a right-hand draw.

He will carry his longbow in his left hand.

KyN/cmm

A detailed character description gives Robin Hood an identity for CONQUESTS OF THE LONGBOW. *Sierra On-Line, Inc.*

Let's follow a design team working on an adventure game meant for personal computers. At Sierra On-Line in Coarsegold, California, the team has decided to make a game titled CONQUESTS OF THE LONGBOW: THE LEGEND OF ROBIN HOOD. The main character will be Robin, an archer.

First the team writes a *design document* listing all the characteristics of Robin and the world he'll inhabit. It's important that details like clothing, weapons, and architecture be true to the game's historical period. The design document also outlines the plot.

Game designers will do a "spec" (short for specification) for every level of game play. In theater movies, there's one screen with a story on it that everyone sees at the same time. In interactive computer games, the scene of the action changes quickly, from three or four to as many as thirteen different levels, depending on choices the player makes. That's why electronic games are called "interactive"—because the signal you send on a keyboard or with a joystick or a mouse causes a reaction in the image on the screen. Your choices affect what happens to the characters—if you make Robin turn left here, he'll enter the sandstone cave. Or you can make him climb the rampart to the castle.

Everything, including architecture, must be true to a game's historical period. *Sierra On-Line, Inc.*

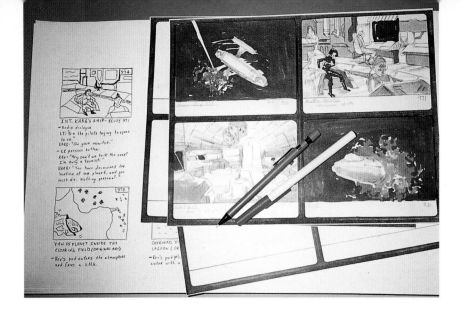

Even though they're roughly sketched, storyboards give a vivid picture of the action to come.
Author photo. Storyboard from Micro-Prose Entertainment Software

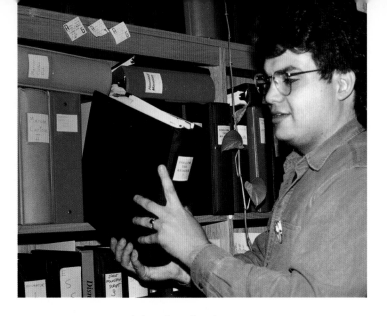

Producer Sam Palahnuk of Disney Software slips a script into a shelf with dozens of other thick game scripts. *Author photo*

Next, the designers team up with artists to sketch a storyboard. Different game manufacturers use different kinds of storyboards. Some are a series of roughly drawn scenes with text and dialogue along the side. Others look like blueprints—on a single sheet, they show all the levels of screen play.

At some companies, a script is written before a storyboard is drawn; other companies write the script afterward. A game script can run anywhere from fifty to one hundred pages in length. It is seldom considered finished until every last detail of the game has been completed. Team members may add to the script or change it anytime, all the way to the end.

Although team members have a lot of input, every part of a game project is managed by a single individual—the producer. This is the person with creative control, who works with all the departments, coordinates their efforts, and tries to keep the game's development on schedule. And on budget!

The producer also verifies that story action fits the character. A producer at Disney Software says, "My job is to make sure that our characters are not mistreated, that they never do something in the game that they wouldn't do in their normal roles. For instance, we can't see Mickey Mouse carrying a gun around, or Ariel the mermaid climbing out of the water without legs."

Once all the preliminary details have been mapped, listed, checked, scripted, and drawn, the game is ready to be put together.

A box cover may be a player's first contact with a game. It needs to convey the "feel" of what the game's about. *Sierra On-Line, Inc.*

21

Artist Mike Gibson lays out his pencil work prior to painting.
Author photo

MAKING IT

Chapter 3

Step three in game making is *programming*. Artists, animators, and programmers all take part in this process.

Different companies use different methods to make screen images. Most often, artists begin by drawing, in pencil, the game characters as they were described in the design documents. Each picture they draw will become one frame of animation—the technical name for a frame is *cel*. The artist draws one cel after another to show consecutive motion as a character climbs or runs or jumps. But only a few major points in each movement have to be drawn, because the computer can fill in the rest. Then, with paint and brushes, the artist colors the figures.

Background art can be detailed and ornate, because backgrounds don't change so often. Foreground figures move constantly.
Author photo. Image by MicroProse Entertainment Software

Backgrounds are also drawn and painted. Because backgrounds don't move around on the screen, they can be quite detailed and elaborate. Since the character images *do* move, they need to be kept simple, because movement requires so many more drawings. And it needs a lot of computer storage space—computers and video-game decks have to store all the instructions to control every single pixel on a screen, and to check them about twenty times per second. (A pixel, short for picture element, is the smallest dot or square you can see on a screen. Look closely at your television screen, and notice how many dots there are.)

After the pictures have been sketched and painted, they're scanned into a computer. A scanner is a piece of equipment that analyzes tiny points of color on a picture, and codes each point into an electrical signal the computer can read.

Game images may be created by methods other than hand drawing. In the clay stop-motion method, sculptors model small-sized clay figures of the game characters. Each figure is set up under lights and photographed. Then the position of the figure is changed just a little bit—an arm or leg is bent, the head barely turned—and it's photographed again. Eventually, all the photos are strung together in sequence and coded into the computer (digitized). The play of light and shadow on them makes their images seem very real.

Clay figures are photographed and then digitized into a program. The play of light and shadow on their features makes them look realistic as they move in the game.
Sierra On-Line, Inc.

When live actors are filmed against a blue background, they seem to be moving in empty space.
Sierra On-Line, Inc.

In a similar way, live actors are sometimes videotaped in front of a blue screen. Because blue doesn't show up on tape or film, the actors seem to be moving in empty space. After the footage gets digitized into the computer, background images are put into the empty space. Since all the scenes were acted out by real people, the subtle movements of their hands and feet and hair and bodies make the computerized figures lifelike. Next, computer artists take over—they add color and adjust the images, pixel by pixel, until they get the look they want.

With every passing year since their invention, computers have become more powerful, able to take over many of the tedious tasks that programmers once had to do. In the most advanced system, developed by 3DO, an artist can draw a single image of a character standing upright, and instruct the computer to make the character bend left or right or stretch in any direction. Previously, the artist would have had to draw step-by-step pictures of the character performing these motions, and then store each picture in the software program.

At MicroProse, animators use a computer paint program to enhance the filmed images of live actors. They're doing pure animation, without any background. *Author photo*

Today's computers can tip images end over end, flop them into reverse, zoom in close up or back away for a more distant perspective. By making objects transparent, they can let you see what's behind them. And the objects can be bigger and more detailed than "sprites"—the small, blocky-looking images that flit across screens trying to zap your player.

After the artists and animators are well along in their work, programmers gather up the script, the background paintings, and the animation, and begin linking everything together. The programmers use special computer languages that require a few years of study to master. Most game software (programs on compact disks, cartridges, or floppy disks) gets written in a language called C.

Today's powerful computers can create layers of objects, one above the other, and let you see right through them. *The 3DO Company*

Most game programmers were game players when they were children. That's how they got interested in programming. *Author photo*

On a keyboard, Ken Lagace can make all kinds of realistic sounds, in addition to music. The keyboard connects directly to the computer.
Author photo

Meanwhile, other programmers are working on sound. In addition to musical backgrounds, games have noises to go with all the action—explosions, footsteps, water splashing, somebody falling down, and so on. Since compact disks can hold so much information, their sound tracks are filled with realistic audio effects, musical and otherwise. Cartridges and floppy disks are more limited: all their sounds—even gunshots—are most often produced on a music keyboard.

All sound effects have to be heard at the exact split second the action happens. In computer coding, "split second" is a literal term, because each second is split into sixty separate segments. Ken Lagace, a sound engineer at MicroProse in Baltimore, Maryland, says, "Hear that?—it's a sword clinking! It's a very high sound, so I have to put a number in the program that will make a high sound, followed by a low sound—the clink of a sword along with the thud of metal. I chop it very short—thirty-sixtieths of a second. I have to dissect every noise in the whole game that way, and then put the right numbers into the registers of the sound-making computer hardware to get the exact sounds I want."

As the sound engineer works, other programmers clean up each cel in the screen images, one by one, taking out any pixels that don't belong there. They continue to adjust and tighten their codes until they think they have a perfect game.

They're usually mistaken. Testers will soon discover every imperfection. Testers have been known to play the game 400 or 500 times, just to look for errors, or "bugs."

Testers do everything they can think of to try to make the game malfunction, treating it much worse than any game player would ever dream of doing. If they succeed in wrecking the game, back it goes to the programmers, who have to fix it—debug it. All this means it's not very likely a real player will be able to damage a game in normal play.

Looking for bugs, testers play games for hours, days, and weeks at a time. If they can't wreck a game, nobody can! *Author photo*

Every game player's dream is to be asked to try out a new game proto-type—no quarters required! All you have to do is tell what you like—or don't like—about the games.
Author photo. Game by MP Game Technologies, Inc.

If the game has been created for an arcade, complex electronic parts are assembled and fitted into a cabinet. The cabinet can be haphazardly constructed out of plywood—it doesn't matter, because it's just a prototype (test model). Later on, the real cabinets will be nicely finished. The model is taken to a nearby shopping mall, where kids are invited to try out the game for free. No quarters required!

David Fike of MP Game Technologies, Inc., describes the scene this way: "The kids know that this is a test, because we hang a sign on it that says, 'NEW GAME. TEST.' To get feedback when they come off the game, we ask them, 'How'd you like it? What did you like best about it? What's good? What's bad?' It's amazing how quickly the kids adapt to a new game, how quickly they can assess it and give us useful evaluations."

Arcade game makers need answers to such questions as whether the monitor is too high, or the foot pedal is too recessed, or the action starts out too slowly, or if the game has drawbacks that might make future players reluctant to drop quarters into the slot.

When everything in a brand-new game checks out, it's time to get the game into the hands of the players.

Author photo. Game by KONAMI
AMERICA, Inc.

Author photo

Magazines, manuals, and other publications help game players. If they don't help enough, you can call a game counselor.   *Author photo*

AN INSIDE LOOK

Chapter 4

The fifth and final stage in the development of a game is to *maintain* it. That means to support the needs of the player.

Most game manufacturers have a staff of counselors who answer questions about games—questions that are either phoned in or mailed in. A player will call and say, "I'm in level three, and I can't get past this one spot. How do I do it?"

With courteous, free, and accurate advice, the counselor talks the player through the obstacle. As they discuss different strategies, the counselor suggests tips, tricks, and techniques that will help the player move toward the game's goal.

Floppy disks, shown outside their protective jackets, are coated with magnetic material. A read/write head in the disk drive touches the surface of the disk to retrieve electronic information.
Author photo

When a player gets hopelessly stuck or messed up in a game, it's natural to blame the game itself, or maybe the equipment, including the cartridge, disk, computer, control deck, joystick, or just about everything except the table the components are sitting on. But almost always, the problem stems from player error rather than equipment failure.

With a computer game, if something weird happens on your screen, it's probably because you've punched the wrong key or put a jack into the wrong port. After all, a computer is merely a piece of machinery that can only follow the instructions you give it when you nudge a joystick, fire a button, or roll a mouse.

Slip a floppy disk (floppy refers to its flexibility) into a computer disk drive, and this is what happens:

A drive motor spins the disk inside its square protective jacket. While it spins, a magnetic head in the disk drive reads information that has been magnetically coded and stored on the disk's glossy surface. This program information is transferred into the computer's memory.

In this particular computer—a 286 IBM clone—the central processing unit is located underneath the power supply. *Author photo*

OVERHEAD VIEW

DISK CONTROLLER

POWER SUPPLY

5.25-INCH FLOPPY DISK DRIVE

RIBBON CABLES

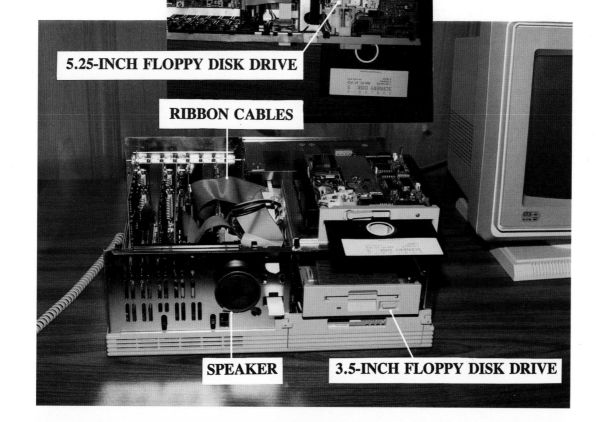

SPEAKER

3.5-INCH FLOPPY DISK DRIVE

A compact disk works similarly to a magnetic disk, except that the coded information on its surface is read by a laser beam. The coded numbers tell the computer which pixels on the screen should be lighted up and which should not—a one means "light the pixel" and a zero means "don't light it." Extra sets of code numbers indicate color.

The computer looks for input from several sources, one of which is the joystick. If you push a button on the joystick, the computer instantly senses this new input and responds to it on the screen. The response happens in milliseconds, which to the computer is a very long segment of time but is too fast to even register in your brain.

The game's software reads signals, like the ones from the joystick, at least ten times per second, and adjusts the screen images in the way the signals tell it to. The joystick doesn't communicate directly with the display (screen image)—it communicates with the central program that's running inside the computer.

Inside a joystick, simple switches send signals to the computer's central processing unit. *Author photo*

In computer games, and in video games, too, a lot of memory gets used up in the fast-paced motion of the figures. Every time a character moves, even if it's only a hand or foot, the movement requires several cels (frames, drawings). Information for each cel has to be stored in the computer's memory. The more memory a computer has, the bigger the program it can handle, which means the screen action can be faster and the quality of the pictures can be better. The latter, though, may not always be needed in the game characters themselves.

Sam Palahnuk, a producer at Disney Software, says, "If you detail a character highly, you use up incredible amounts of program storage. And it isn't always necessary. When you study animation, you learn that the human eye is much more interested in movement than in detail. If you view a series of related pictures [frames] in rapid succession, your brain interprets them as continuous motion."

With video games, you usually use a controller or a mouse instead of a joystick. All three send signals in pretty much the same way.
Nintendo of America, Inc. ©1992. Nintendo products used by permission.

Super Nintendo's MARIO PAINT lets you create your own animation, using from four to nine frames that play in sequence. You can also compose songs on MARIO PAINT, and color your own graphics.
Author photo. Screen image™ © 1994 Nintendo. All rights reserved.

The more frequently an image is updated on the screen, the smoother the motion looks. "Frames per second" is the term for the number of times a screen image gets updated. Television pictures change at the rate of 30 frames per second. The new 3DO Interactive Multiplayer system also works at 30 frames per second, but most computer and video games aren't that swift. Kerry Wilkinson, a software engineer at MP Game Technologies, Inc., says, "Twenty frames per second is pretty good motion. The high teens—we can live with that. But when you start getting down to ten or twelve frames per second, especially if things are moving fast, it looks pretty cartoonish. You want

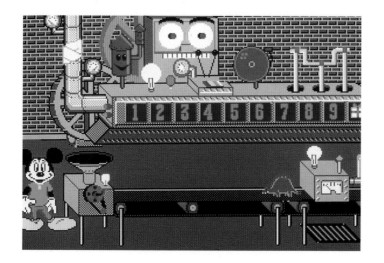

to suspend reality in a game; you don't want players to feel like they're watching these things being drawn on the screen."

The look of a game also depends on the amount of color on a screen. Most games come in two versions—EGA and VGA. EGA stands for *Enhanced Graphics Array*; it allows 16 colors to appear on the screen at the same time, out of a total of 64 different available colors on the program's palette. VGA—for *Video Graphics Array*—puts 256 colors on the screen at one time, out of 262,144 possible colors.

A third version—the next step up—is called Super VGA, or just True Color, with a total palette of 16,777,216 colors! It's hard to believe that human eyes can notice such an enormous range of hues, but that's what you see on movie screens, in the

On a computer screen, pixels are arranged in rows, like the squares on graph paper. The more pixels on a screen, the smoother and sharper the images will look. *Author photo*

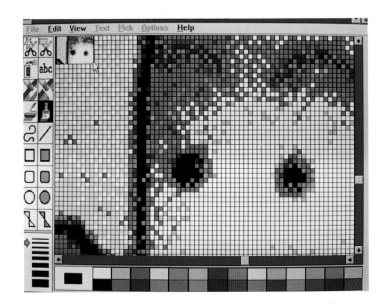

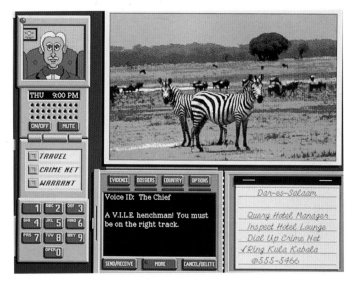

This CD-ROM version of **WHERE IN THE WORLD IS CARMEN SANDIEGO** has excellent high-resolution images.
Broderbund Software, Inc.

shadings that vary from totally dark to totally bright. Now you can see them in advanced video-game systems, too.

Resolution is another factor in how good a screen image looks. Resolution is determined by the number of pixels in a screen display—the more pixels, the sharper the image. A standard TV image has more than 200,000 pixels in each frame. Low-resolution images, with fewer pixels, look jagged on the edges. Here's why:

If you look through a wire window screen, the scene you see outside seems divided into tiny squares. Display images on monitors are divided up the same way, with pixels lined up side by side in rows, and the rows stacked one above the other from bottom to top of the screen.

Each pixel lights up in only one single color at one time, but when it receives a signal, it can change to any other color in the palette. Put together, the pixels create a mosaic effect, like a picture you might draw by filling in the squares on graph paper. Divide those graph-paper squares by four and color them in, and you can give the mosaic much greater detail, or resolution, and the edges will look smoother.

If more pixels are lighted up, and more characters are filling the screen, and the game is moving very fast, a great deal of information will need to be stored. Since compact disks can store so much information, games on CDs can have beautiful, highly detailed images, as well as great sound.

The Super Nintendo Entertainment System (NES), Sega's Genesis, and NEC's TurboGrafx-16 all have 16-bit central processing units. The original systems from these manufacturers had 8-bit CPUs—this term tells you the amount of information that can be processed at the same instant. An 8-bit

In the Nintendo Entertainment System (8-bit), the central processing unit—CPU—is on the right. The picture processing unit—PPU—is beneath the game pack.
Author photo. Nintendo products used by permission.

Inside a Super Nintendo cartridge is an integrated microcircuit. Its connector pins transfer information to the CPU.
Author photo. Nintendo products used by permission.

An integrated microcircuit fits snugly inside a Super NES Game Pack, with the pins projecting outside.
Author photo. Nintendo products used by permission.

system (stands for 2 to the 8th power, meaning $2 \times 2 \times 2 \times 2 \times 2 \times 2 \times 2 \times 2$) provides 16 colors and an animation speed of about 100,000 pixels per second. A 16-bit system (2 to the 16th power) has 256 colors and reaches an animation speed of about a million pixels per second. Animation speed is the number of pixels on screen multiplied by frames per second. In the latest video-game technology, animation speed can reach more than 36 million pixels per second.

With most video games, the software programs come inside game cartridges, and the entertainment systems themselves function as computers. Control decks, like computers, have *Central Processing Units* inside them, as well as *Picture Processing Units*. A CPU—the brains of the unit—gets its instructions from the controller. The PPU takes digital information from both the CPU and the game pack, and converts the information into video signals.

Inside a game-pack cartridge, if you opened it (and you'd better not if you ever want to use that game pack again!) are integrated microcircuits, sandwiched on silicon wafers, attached to connector pins. When a game pack is inserted into a control deck, the pins plug in, letting information pass from the integrated circuits to the central processing unit and the picture processing unit.

If all the above technical information seems way too complicated, don't worry. You don't have to understand any of it to have fun playing games. But if you'd like to become a game designer or programmer or producer someday, you'll need to learn this, and more (see Chapter Six).

Seta U.S.A. lets you sample game design in its WIZARD OF OZ game for Nintendo. Traci McCarty says, "We've left some of the developers' tools in the game so the kids can make changes—like the color—if they want to." Players can even change the function of the buttons on the game controller. "The kids who are playing the games now . . . ," says Traci, "these kids are going to be the developers in the next five or ten years. We want to give them a little taste of it now."

Seta U.S.A. leaves developers' tools inside the WIZARD OF OZ program to let you control the color. *Author photo. Screen images by Seta U.S.A., Inc.*

Games of the punch-and-kick variety have been a mainstay of arcades from the beginning.
Author photo. Street Fighter II Champion Edition™ is a trademark of Capcom Co., Ltd. © 1992.

AT THE ARCADE Chapter 5

Twenty-some years ago, a graduate student at the University of Utah created simple games on the university's eight million dollar computer. His name was Nolan Bushnell. In 1976 Mr. Bushnell, no longer a student, invented a game that could be played in arcades; he called it PONG. That game, and other early arcade games like PAC-MAN, became such hits that the mechanisms kept getting jammed from too many quarters being stuffed into the slots.

But that was small change compared to the $7 billion—each year—that Americans eagerly poured into coin-op games by the 1990s. By then arcade games had become incredibly sophisticated, compared to those groundbreakers PONG and PAC-MAN. Each passing year has brought not only new games, but new *varieties* of games, in addition to the standard punch-and-kicks and shooters that have been around almost since the beginning, played mostly by boys.

Lately, more girls have discovered the excitement of the arcades, particularly of road-racing games, mazes, and simulators. At Space Center Houston, the official visitors' center of NASA's Johnson Space Center, girls are as likely as boys to successfully pilot a space shuttle in a realistic simulated landing. It's so tricky to maneuver that U.S. astronauts who have actually flown in space have had trouble landing the shuttle on the simulated runway. They've been known to crash!

That's the good thing about electronic games—you can crash and burn without getting a scratch. In arcades all over the world, kids who won't be old enough to drive a real car for years can grip a steering wheel, stomp down on an accelerator pedal, and speed around hairpin turns. Piloting flight simulators, kids—and more than a few grown-ups—whirl and dip in actual motion while they fire missiles at enemy fighter planes on the screen.

Girls seem drawn to city-building games, mazes, and simulators like this one at Space Center Houston.

No matter how young you are, you can fly planes in an arcade, as fast as you want to go. Crash, and you start all over again. *Author photo*

Want to find out if you'd be good at golf? Pick up a real club and slam a real ball, straight at a screen. Three cameras measure the speed and angle of your flying ball, both before and after it hits the screen. And look! Onto the projected image of a real golf course, there goes your ball, soaring, falling, bouncing on the green. A computer and a mirror system calculate the trajectory of the ball and project its image as it curves and lands, so you can see exactly where you hit it.

Or you can have an encounter with movie actors as they play their roles and you play yours. You're part of the screen action. Only, all you get to do is shoot the bad guys. If you shoot and miss, they look you right in the eye and tell you, out loud so everyone can hear, that you'd better improve your aim.

Slam a ball onto the Pebble Beach Golf Course, or the next best thing to it—its screen image. Computers track the ball you hit and accurately map its trajectory. *Author photo. Game by Par T Golf*

Play in a movie with live actors. If you shoot and miss, the screen action will be different than if you score a hit. *Author photo. Screen image by American Laser Games*

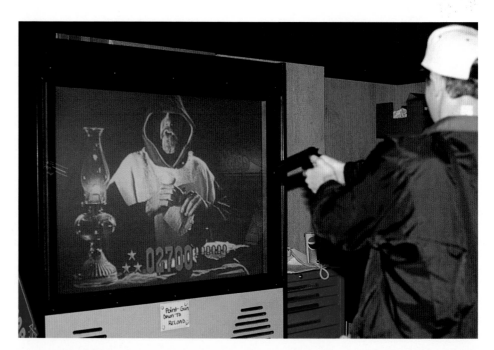

48

Go ahead, try to grab a Time Traveler—they're out there in the open. Your hand will go right through them because they're made of light. *Sega of America, Inc.*

Next, play a game with the little people who aren't there, in Sega's TIME TRAVELER HOLOGRAM. The manufacturers have taken some liberties with the name of this game, because a real hologram uses lasers, and TIME TRAVELER doesn't— it's all done with mirrors. Reflecting light, special, black, spherical mirrors create an amazing three-dimensional illusion. As you reach out to touch Kyi-La, Princess of the Galactic Federation, your hand goes right through her! As real as she looks, she's only made of light, as are all the characters in TIME TRAVELER.

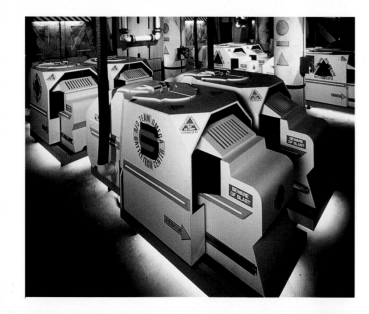

At Battletech, you're encased in a pod. Four to a team, in four separate pods, you battle other Battlemechs, each one thirty feet tall. Or so they appear.
Virtual World Entertainments, Inc.

Zoom ahead to the thirty-first century in Chicago's Battletech Center. There you can enter one of sixteen stationary pods that are cockpits for Battlemechs, nicknamed 'mechs. Close the sliding cover and you're encased in the virtual-world cockpit of your own 'mech, which you control with a throttle, foot pedals, and a three-button joystick.

A different virtual reality experience—more like the scientific kind still mostly in laboratories—is called VIRTUALITY. To play, you stand on a platform, and a ring is lowered around you at waist level. Headgear that resembles an elongated motorcycle helmet keeps you from seeing anything except the images projected onto a screen inside the helmet.

Inside your pod, you follow the action on two screens. The upper screen is your window to the virtual world; the lower displays radar information, long-range scanners, armor status, and other functions.
Virtual World Entertainments, Inc.

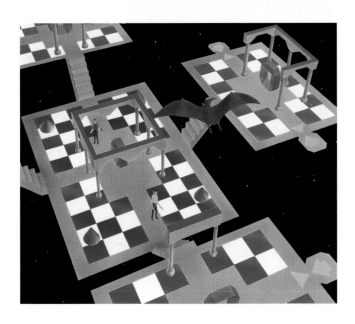

From this two-dimensional photo, it's hard to imagine how immersed a player feels in three-dimensional **VIRTUALITY**.
Horizon Entertainment. VIRTUALITY is a Trademark of W Industries.

Raise and lower your head, or turn all the way around, and the images shift, too, just as they would if you were turning in the real world. The images may be chunky and a bit cartoonish, but you hardly notice because this virtual world looks entirely three-dimensional. Colors are vivid and luminous, and the action is nonstop as enemies stalk you.

VIRTUALITY's graphics are simple, but they'll improve when technology advances. For now, the excitement comes from being immersed in a world where you can't see your real hand in front of your face—only your virtual hand, rendered into graphic images by a computer.

In **VIRTUALITY**, a player ducks, swings arms, and whirls around, fighting enemies that no outside observer can see.
Horizon Entertainment. VIRTUALITY is a Trademark of W Industries.

Roberta Williams and her husband, Ken, own Sierra On-Line, Inc. Started in 1980 on their kitchen table, Sierra now has a staff of 500.
Sierra On-Line, Inc.

DESIGNING PEOPLE

Chapter 6

Roberta Williams may have authored more computer games than anyone else in the world. She's best known for her KING'S QUEST series. With her husband, Ken, Roberta Williams co-founded Sierra On-Line, Inc. How does she feel about the work she does? In her own words:

I consider myself a writer first and foremost. I know I design computer games, but the types of games that I do are adventure games—basically interactive fiction. They're pretty much storylike. To me, just creating stories that come to life, and knowing that people are enjoying what I create, gives me by far the most satisfaction.

The KING'S QUEST series is a chronicle of old-fashioned values and heroism and truth. People find they can win by using their heads, and through good acts, hard work, and honesty. They find that intelligence and kindness will win out where violence will not.

Like many people currently creating games, Darlene Waddington learned by doing. Her college degree in broadcast communications helped, but on-the-job experience turned her into a producer.   *Author photo*

Darlene Waddington, an associate producer at Walt Disney Computer Software, Inc., had no notion during her college years that she'd one day be creating electronic games. She tells how she does it:

I always do "what-ifs"—what if you turn going to the grocery store into a game? What if you were broke, with no money at all, and you were left downtown; how would you get home? It's thinking creatively, looking at situations that you're in. . . . Even when you're playing a game, you can ask yourself, "What if the hero's arms were tied behind his back? How would the game be played then?"

As a producer, I'm in charge of finding the team of people to work on the product, in charge of the concept as a whole. In general, I keep an eye on everything. In particular, I like to design my games, too. I like the creative control—I tend to get involved very deeply.

At Disney Software, Scott Wolf and Sam Palahnuk test a new learning game, FOLLOW THE READER.
Author photo

At Disney Software, Sam Palahnuk and Scott Wolf are working on FOLLOW THE READER, a learning game for young children. Sam is the producer, Scott the assistant producer.

Scott: When you actually test a game, a lot of it is exploring every single option the game offers. I've been playing this for two hours now and I still haven't seen everything in it. This is a game to help kids from kindergarten to third grade learn to read.

Sam: We provide variety so kids won't get tired of it in half an hour.

Scott: Even if you choose the same options, sometimes different things will appear—whenever you look in the mirror, you'll see different reflections. Based on the choices you make, you can't lose. In this game there's no way to lose.

Sam: I enjoy doing the educational games. I was a very frustrated student—I didn't like school very much. So it's a real opportunity for me to make software that I know I would like if I were a kid again. Because when kids fall behind in class, it's hard work to catch up; but if they're ahead, they're bored. With a computer, the blessing is that the computer keeps pace with the child, not the other way around.

Bernice Stafford is product marketing manager at Jostens Learning Corporation. In educational computer-software companies, women fill a majority of management positions. *Jostens Learning Corporation*

Bernice Stafford is product marketing manager at Jostens Learning Corporation. She manages a full curriculum of sixty-five computer stories, starting at prekindergarten, reaching to grade three. According to Ms. Stafford:

There's a mutual admiration society in this business. We admire the creativity of Sierra, and we tell them so. And Disney has taken the content and done such wonderful things with it.

In the educational side of computer programs, outside the games arena, there are probably more women than men. They began in education, and then their enthusiasm about technology took them to a second career.

I came into this business from curiosity. I'd started out with Head Start, where I learned the elements of a good childhood education program. Then I spent four years with the Ministry of Education in Saudi Arabia. That's where I got my baptism by fire with computers—I bought my first one and learned to program it, self-taught. And I started thinking, How might the computer revolutionize American education?

Since then, in classrooms, I've seen the most astounding things going on with computer programs. Educational games do have a strong place today.

Kerry Wilkinson (left) and Mike McDonald, software engineers at MP Game Technologies, Inc., would like to see arcade games become more thoughtful, to involve brains and strategy rather than just joystick manipulation. *David S. Nolan*

Kerry Wilkinson and Mike McDonald are software engineers at MP Game Technologies, Inc. Both consider themselves lucky to do the kind of work they do:

Mike: I've always loved computer games; I've loved simulations. I wanted to be a pilot, but when I got glasses, that was it for me. And so the next best thing was trying to do something like this, getting involved with simulation. . . . Hey, where else can you play games for a living?

Kerry: The fact that it's entertainment makes it harder in some ways, because there's always that nebulous thing which is "fun"—you know when you're having it, but what exactly does it entail? What makes something fun, and not another thing?

The rewarding aspect of it is when you actually hear a kid talking about a game that you've done. You hear eight- or ten-year-old kids laughing and pointing things out on the arcade screen—it's a big feedback, it's a big kick. It's not a conceited thing; it's just nice to know that you had a part in their enjoyment.

Mike: We're poised to do virtual reality. It will be a feeling that nobody's ever had before with computer games—where it won't be your physical strength that matters, but your mind! That's the real strength. Your mind.

Glossary

animator an artist who draws pictures, in sequence, of a character's movements

bit the smallest unit of information in a computer, written as a 1 or a 0. Short for "binary digit"

C a particular computer language. Some others are BASIC, PASCAL, and FORTRAN.

cartridge a plug-in unit that holds a software program

CD, or **compact disk** 5¼-inch platter holding digital data produced with optical read/write technology. It has vast storage capacity.

CD-I the interactive capability of a compact disk

CD-ROM a compact disk with read-only memory: you can read data from it, but you can't record on it

cel a single picture in an animation sequence

cinematography the art of photographing movies

concept the overall idea or theme of a story

connector pins solid wire lines that carry signals between electronic devices. They allow you to make and break connections.

control deck a custom-designed, mass-marketed computer that connects to a television set to display interactive video games

CPU central processing unit; the part of a computer that interprets and acts on instructions from input devices

digitize to code with the 1s and 0s that computers can read

disk drive a computer component for mass storage of electronic files and programs

display a visual representation of electronic information on a screen

EGA enhanced graphics array; EGA, VGA, and Super VGA refer to the number of colors on a screen and the quality of the image

environment a mode of operation; a system defined by computer hardware, software, and intended use

floppy disk a flat, round, thin, magnetically coated plate that stores information; can be both written to and read from

frame the unchanging image that fills a monitor for one split second

game pack a hard plastic container that holds a video-game software program

genre type, category

hardware physical components that make up a computer system

high density a greater capacity for data on the same size storage device

hologram a three-dimensional image that may be computer-generated. It can appear to exist in empty space.

integrated microcircuit a complete electronic circuit contained on a tiny silicon chip

interactive a software environment that requires and responds to human input

jack a connector

joystick an input device that uses a lever control to send directions to software

laser an intense, very narrow beam of light formed by concentrated light waves

malfunction a failure in operation

memory the storage facilities of a computer

millisecond one one-thousandth of a second

monitor device for viewing your interactions with the computer

mouse   a roller-ball device that provides input to the computer. It allows the user to move a cursor, point to a symbol on the computer screen, or key-click to start a function.

perspective   the view from a particular place

pixel   the smallest dot of light on a computer monitor or video screen. Short for "picture element"

platform   a hardware or software environment

point of view   the view through a particular individual's eyes

port   a place to plug in an input device such as a mouse or a joystick

PPU   picture processing unit; a component that reproduces the game graphics

program   instructions that cause a computer to process information

programmer   a person who writes codes that instruct a computer to do a specific job

prototype   the first version or model of any system ready for testing

resolution   the quality and clarity of a screen image, generally based on the number of pixels in a display. The higher the number of pixels, the better the image looks.

scanner   an optical device that can recognize visual symbols

script   written dialogue and directions that take a story from beginning to end

simulator   a configuration of hardware and software that provides the user with an environment like the real world

software   electronic programs that direct the hardware to perform its various functions

specification   description of requirements for a product

sprites   small, fast-moving, animated figures without much detail

stereo-optic   two optical paths that blend together to create a three-dimensional image

storage   the ability of a computer device to accept electronic information, hold it, and deliver it on demand

storyboard   rough drawings that show how a story will develop

Super VGA, or **True Color**   the highest quality of color that can appear in a screen image

VGA   video graphics array; see EGA

virtual reality   an environment in which a user can interact from within computer-generated images

zoom   to enlarge or reduce an image on a screen, creating the illusion that it's moving closer or farther away

Index